THIS BOOK BELONGS TO:

_____

To Mum and Dad for all the stories
and to Lou, for always being there for me.

This paperback edition first published in 2018 by Andersen Press Ltd.
First published in Great Britain in 2017 by Andersen Press Ltd.,
20 Vauxhall Bridge Road, London SW1V 2SA.
Copyright © Robert Starling 2017.
The right of Robert Starling to be identified as the author
and illustrator of this work have been asserted by him in
accordance with the Copyright, Designs and Patents Act, 1988.
All rights reserved.
Printed and bound in China.

1 3 5 7 9 10 8 6 4 2

British Library Cataloguing in Publication Data available.
ISBN 978 1 78344 590 5

ROBERT STARLING

FERGAL IS FUMING!

ANDERSEN PRESS

This is Fergal.
What a nice chap!

He's a friendly little fellow.

But when someone
tells him what to do,
Fergal gets very...

very...

ANGRY.

Like when his dad said,
"Fergal, come down for your tea!"

But Fergal wanted to carry on playing.

And then he said
Fergal had to eat all
his vegetables if he
wanted pudding.

Fergal felt fiery.

"It's **not**
FAIR!"

"I don't want to eat my GREEEEENS!!"

So Fergal didn't get any pudding,
and he didn't get any tea, either.

Fergal got in a pickle
on the football pitch.

YOU'RE IN
GOAL!

"It's **not** FAIR!" said Fergal.

"I don't want to go in..."

KAWUMFFF!

"... goal."

His fiery temper got Fergal into trouble all over town.

Wherever he went, Fergal just couldn't keep his cool.

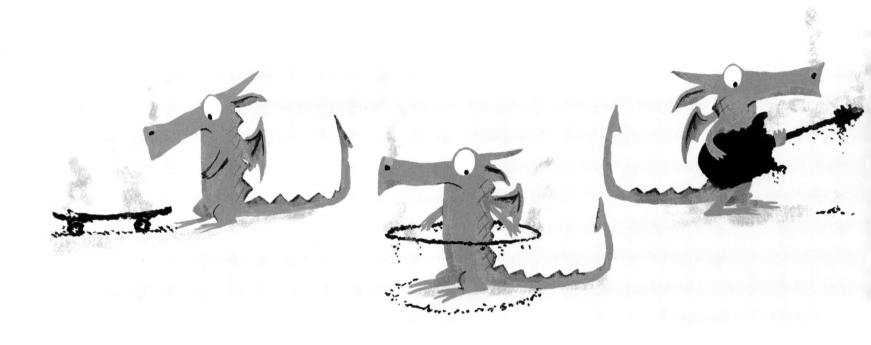

Finally his friends had had enough.

"Everyone's ignoring me, Mum," said Fergal.

"It's **not** FAIR!"

"Well Fergal, dinner is in the bin, Bear's buns are burnt and no one can play football, and that's not fair."

"We all get fiery," sighed Mum, "but we find a way
to cool down. My trick is to count to ten."

The next day, Fergal felt fiery again.

"That's **not**..."

But then he remembered his mum's trick...

"ONE! TWO! THREE. Four. Five..."

... and he didn't feel so fiery.

It had worked!

Fergal noticed lots of animals had their own way to cool down.

When Crow felt fiery, he told his friends about it.

When Fox felt fiery,

he watched the sunset.

Wolf always found a nice
quiet spot and made a
BIG NOISE!

AWOOOOOOOOOOOOOOOO

Cat lay back and had a really good stretch.

And then there was Hare: whizzing about
stopped her feeling fiery in the first place.

Now Fergal had lots of ways to
cool down, and when he didn't waste
his fire on being angry...

... he found there were much more interesting things to do with it.